A Note to Parents an D1309863

DK READERS is a compelling programme for beginning readers, designed in conjunction with leading literacy experts, including Maureen Fernandes, B.Ed (Hons). Maureen has spent many years teaching literacy, both in the classroom and as a specialist in schools.

Beautiful illustrations and superb full-colour photographs combine with engaging, easy-to-read stories to offer a fresh approach to each subject in the series. Each DK READER is guaranteed to capture a child's interest while developing his or her reading skills, general knowledge and love of reading.

The five levels of DK READERS are aimed at different reading abilities, enabling you to choose the books that are exactly right for your child:

Pre-level 1: Learning to read
Level 1: Beginning to read
Level 2: Beginning to read alone
Level 3: Reading alone
Level 4: Proficient readers

The "normal" age at which a child begins to read can be anywhere from three to eight years old. Adult participation through the lower levels is very helpful for providing encouragement, discussing storylines and sounding out unfamiliar words.

No matter which level you select, you can be sure that you are helping your child learn to read, then read to learn!

LONDON, NEW YORK, MUNICH,
MELBOURNE and DELHI

Senior Editor Helen Murray
Designer Lauren Rosier
Managing Editor Laura Gilbert
Design Manager Nathan Martin
Publishing Manager Julie Ferris
Art Director Ron Stobbart
Publishing Director Simon Beecroft
Pre-Production Producer Siu Yin Chan
Producer Louise Daly

Designed and edited by Tall Tree Ltd
Designer Malcolm Parchment
Editor Catherine Saunders

Reading Consultant
Maureen Fernandes

This edition published for The Book People,
Hall Wood Avenue, Haydock, St. Helens WA11 9UL

This edition published in 2013
First published in Great Britain in 2012 by
Dorling Kindersley Limited
80 Strand, London WC2R 0RL
Penguin Group (UK)

Slipcase Unique ID: 001–196366–Jul/13

LEGO, the LEGO logo, the Brick and the Knob
configurations are trademarks of the LEGO Group.
© 2013 The LEGO Group
Produced by Dorling Kindersley
under license from the LEGO Group.

A CIP catalogue record for this book is
available from the British Library

ISBN: 978-1-4093-3792-8

Colour reproduction by Alta Image
Printed and bound in China by L.Rex Printing Co. Ltd.

Discover more at
www.dk.com
www.LEGO.com

Contents

DK READERS

BEGINNING TO READ ALONE

2

Let's go Riding

Written by Catherine Saunders

Animal friends

Olivia, Emma, Stephanie, Mia, and Andrea are best friends and they love hanging out together. The girls have many hobbies, but they share a love of animals.

Stephanie

Andrea

Puppy

Rabbit

The girls care about all animals. However, two of them share a passion for one special type of animal – horses! Come on, let's go riding with horse-crazy Mia and Emma.

Olivia

Bird

Emma

Mia

Hedgehog

Cat

Mia and Bella

Mia is an outdoor girl. She loves camping, canoeing, and riding her horse, Bella. In her spare time, Mia helps the Heartlake City vet care for sick or injured animals.

Mane

Carrot

Bella

Mia's dream job would definitely involve animals. She might become a vet, an animal psychologist, or work in a pet rescue centre.

Hay

Emma and Robin

Emma loves decorating, drawing and designing clothes. She likes to share her talents with her friends by giving them, or their bedrooms, makeovers.

Emma dreams of becoming a fashion designer or an interior decorator one day.

Emma always seems to know what's in fashion, and what isn't. But there's one thing that will always be in fashion for Emma – her horse Robin. She thinks Robin is simply perfect.

Bridle

Robin

Saddle

Tail

Brush

Hoof

Stirrup

Comb

Horse show

Emma loves horseback riding and her favourite part is jumping. Emma and Robin are a great team and they often enter horse jumping competitions.

Katharina

Gate

Today, Emma and Robin are travelling to a horse show. They plan to win the jumping contest. Emma leads Robin into his blue horse trailer. He travels in style!

Horse trailer

Ramp

Emma is getting Robin ready for the competition. First, she gives him a long drink of water and some carrots so that he has enough energy to jump high over all the fences.

Saddle

Riding hat

Riding boots

Horses love eating carrots. Robin is so gentle and friendly that Emma can feed him carrots straight from her hand.

Bridle

Reins

Next, it's time for Emma to put on her riding hat and boots. Finally, she saddles up Robin. Good luck Emma and Robin!

Emma and Robin have won the competition! Robin cleared all the jumps. Emma is so proud of her clever horse.

Bow

Winner's rosette

Brush

Jumping high
Horse jumping is hard. Emma and Robin must time their jump perfectly so they don't knock the fence down.

Emma pins the blue winner's rosette onto Robin's mane. It's a perfect fashion accessory. Emma cleans and grooms her tired horse. Robin has worked so hard today, but now it's time to go home. Well done Robin, Emma has a special reward for you – some extra carrots!

At the stables

Mia likes to spend as much time as she can with her horse. Every day, after school, she goes to visit Bella at the stables.

Stables

Flag

Horse fan
Katharina would like to be a famous rider or a horse trainer. She has a horse called Niki.

During the school holidays, Mia can spend all day at the stables. Her friend Katharina also likes to spend a lot of time there. Mia sometimes forgets that she needs to hang out with Stephanie, Olivia, Emma and Andrea too. Stephanie jokes that Mia prefers animals to people!

Mia brushes Bella's mane and tail every day. She also makes sure her horse has plenty of fresh hay to eat.

Looking after a horse isn't simple. Every day, Mia must feed Bella, groom her and clean out her stable. It's hard work, but horse-loving Mia doesn't mind.

For Mia, the best part of the day is exercising Bella because that means riding her! Mia and Bella often go for very long rides.

They like to practise cantering in the beautiful countryside around Heartlake City.

Tail

Mane

Grass

It's been another busy day looking after their horses, but Mia and Katharina can finally relax. So, how do the two friends like to spend their free time?

Flag

Stable door

Bella

Niki

Mia and Katharina have spent all day with their horses, but they can't wait to come back tomorrow.

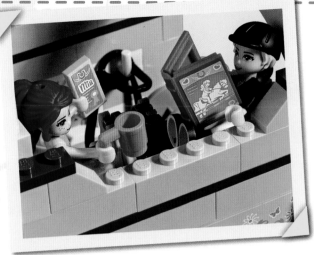

They talk about horses and read horse magazines, of course!

Bella and Niki are happy too. They've had a very exciting day thanks to Mia and Katharina.

Now the sleepy horses are safe and secure in their clean stables.

Water well

Off to the vet

Mia is worried about Bella. Something seems to be wrong with one of her front hooves. Poor Bella is limping, but Mia knows someone who can help: Sophie, the Heartlake City vet.

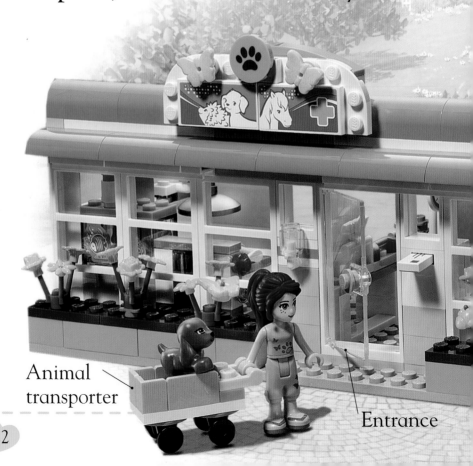

Animal transporter

Entrance

Meet the vet

Sophie is an animal expert. She helps all the sick or injured animals in Heartlake City.

Sophie is also Mia's friend Olivia's aunt. Mia is sure that she'll know exactly what to do for Bella.

Stable

Sophie carefully checks Bella's injured hoof and immediately finds the problem. Bella has a stone in her hoof! The vet very gently removes the stone.

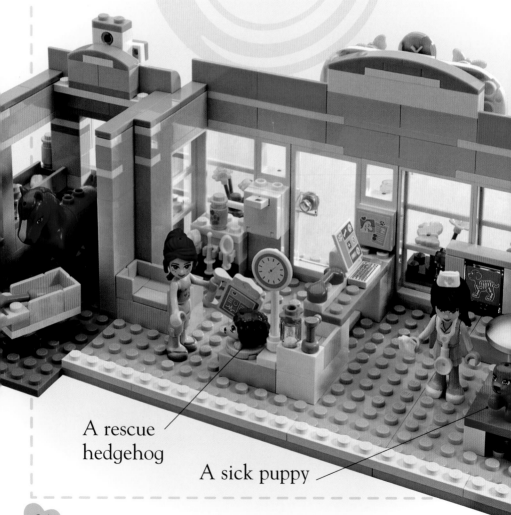

A rescue hedgehog

A sick puppy

Mia loves helping Sophie with the animals.
It's good practice for her future career!

Sophie gives Bella a
carrot for being such a
brave horse. Bella will be
fine now, she just needs to
rest for a while. So, Mia
stays to help Sophie with
the other animals, while
Bella recovers.

Riding camp

Stephanie also loves horses and she has an idea for the perfect summer holiday – riding camp! She invites Emma and her friend Ella to join her.

Old friend
Ella and Stephanie live in different towns, but they email, phone, text or write to each other regularly.

Emma and Ella think it's a wonderful plan. At riding camp they'll be able to go on long horse rides, talk about horses all day and make lots of new, equally horse-mad, friends.
So, the three excited girls set off in their stylish minibus. Riding camp, here they come!

Theresa is an experienced riding instructor and horse expert.

Riding camp is just as much fun as Stephanie, Emma, and Ella thought it would be, but it's hard work too! Theresa, the riding instructor, teaches the girls how to ride horses, how to feed them, and how to care for them.

After their lessons, the girls practise what they have learned in the paddock. By the end of the camp, Stephanie, Emma, and Ella will be expert horse riders!

Robin

Horse cart

Theresa

It's been another fantastic day at riding camp, but Stephanie, Emma and Ella must go home tomorrow. However, Theresa has something extra-special planned for their last night at camp.

Hot chocolate

Campfire

Marshmallow

Emma and Stephanie are too excited to sleep. They can't wait to tell Andrea, Mia and Olivia all about riding camp!

She shows them how to build a campfire and toast marshmallows. As the girls drink hot chocolate, they agree that riding camp has been the best fun they've ever had. They all want to come back next year!

Quiz

1. What colour is Robin's horse box?

2. What is the name of Katharina's horse?

3. How do Mia and Katharina like to relax?

4. What is the name of the Heartlake City vet?

5. Who goes to riding camp with Stephanie and Emma?

1. Blue 2. Niki 3. By reading horse magazines and talking about horses 4. Sophie 5. Ella